Dinosaur Explore

By Jon Michael Pinckney, Jr.

2020 "Dinosaur Explore"

ISBN 978-1-7358268-2-0
For more information on the content of this book, email jmpinckneypublishing@gmail.com

JMPinckney Publishing Company, LLC
104 Berkeley Square Lane
PMB 28
Goose Creek, South Carolina 29445

Illustration and Design
Damith Perera in Sri lanka (Fiverr)

Written by
Kaylona Scott

Printed in the
United States of America.

"Bedtime stories are for babies," Jon said to his Dad.
"Oh, really?! I thought you liked bedtime stories." Dad laughed.

Bedtime stories were a nightly tradition, and Dad knew
when Jon started refusing story-time, it was time for new books.
"So let's plan a trip to Miguel's Book Shop in the morning."

"Yes! Okay, I can't wait to see what he has." Jon smiled.
Jon loved going to Miguel's Book Shop.
Miguel always had cool toys and new books for all the
neighborhood kids to play with in his shop.

"Hey guys, what's up?" Miguels looks up from behind the counter.
Miguels was the perfect place to go on Saturdays.
There was always a STEM workshop, community service event,
or birthday parties. He also had a video game
console set up for kids to try out new games.

Jon spotted Max, his classmate,
putting his name on the list to play the new video game.
"Don't forget, we came for a few new books,"
Dad called over to Jon.
"Sure thing, Dad." Jon dashed over to Max.

"Let's check out the new books while we wait for
our spot on the game." Max suggested.
"Cool, let's check it out." Jon and Max walked over to the
huge bookshelf. There were used books and new releases.
So many different types of books,
but there was one that caught Max's eyes.

"Wow. This looks cool." Max said, holding up a
huge book that was definitely used. The book was heavy and old.
The title Dinosaur Explore shined in gold lettering.
Although it looked old on the outside,
the pages were crisp and vibrant inside.

"PUT 3D GLASSES ON BEFORE PROCEEDING"
projected from the first page.
"What does that say?" Jon leaned to look at the page.
Instructions were printed in fine print followed by a bright command:
Press the yellow stone on the spine, if you dare.

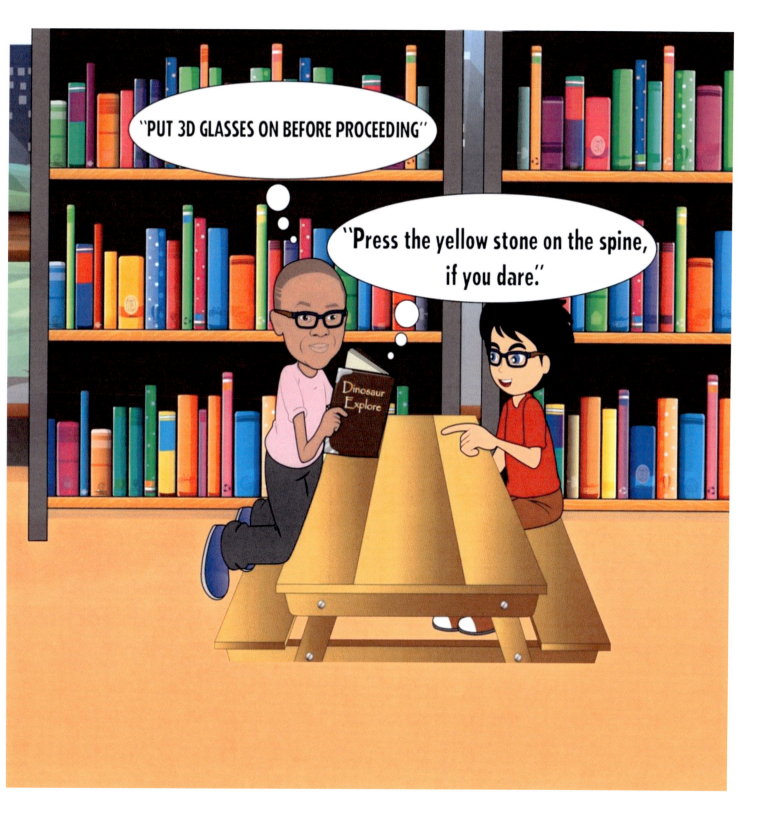

"We do!" Jon and Max said simultaneously.
They let out a big laugh as they pressed the yellow stone embedded into the spine of the huge book. Instantly the room changed drastically to lush green grass covering the ground, and tall plants sprouted around them. In a matter of seconds, the boys were engulfed in a jungle vibrant with life.

"Oh, goodness! Where are we? What's happening?" Jon looked around curiously. "I don't know, dude, but the glasses are not coming off." Jon tried pulling the glasses from his face and realized that Max was indeed telling the truth.

The page flipped to an image of a diplodocus and a riddle. A message appears magically. A tickle will do, may not be the bottom, but the top will do.

"So, are we supposed to tickle the dinosaur? Is this book serious?" Jon looked at Max. Max looks at Jon. The boys scream in shock! "Seems like the only way to get out of this book is through it," Max said. "So where is the Diplodocus? It would be nice to have a map." Standing and looking around, Max realized that they needed more than just the glasses and the book.

"There must be a map." Max said to Jon.
Jon tried looking through the pages, but they didn't budge.
Turning the book to its back cover,
Jon discovered the map in a gold envelope attached.
"I've found it! A map!" Jon excitedly opened the envelope and pulled
a very worn map from it. The map seemed magical in itself, as well.
It showed markings for many dinosaurs, waterfalls, jungles, and such that
seemed alive on paper.

"Where's the Diplodocus?"
Max looked over the map as Jon stood holding it up.
"There! The Diplodocus Den" The boys exclaimed together.

"We don't seem to be too far from their spot on the map.
Let's head this way." Jon enjoyed being a ranger scout but never
really thought he would have to use all those skills until now.
"Uh, Okay, you sure, dude?" Max said nervously.
"I think it's the only way out. We have to work together, okay?"
Jon tried to comfort Max, but deep down, he was scared too.

The boys made their way to the Diplodocus Den.
What they saw shocked them. A huge dinosaur with a long tail and
stubby legs lay resting in the jungle's lush grass.
"This may be the best time to tickle a dinosaur. He's asleep!"
Max whispered.
The boys started at the tail and followed it to the huge body,
then to the Diplodocus's long curvy neck.

"I think we're close. The dinosaur's neck can't be too much longer. Right?"
Max yelled as Jon trod ahead of him. "I think you're right. But wait.
He's starting to move," Jon shouted as he put the book in a
backpack that magically appeared on his back.

The leaves rustled, and the ground began to shake as the
giant dinosaur lifted his huge body from the ground.
The boys jumped on the neck of the Diplodocus.
"HOLD ON TIIIIIIGGGGGHHHHT!" Max screamed!
They were lifted high in the air.

The boys made it to the top of the Diplodocus.
They felt so small sitting on the head of this huge dinosaur
that didn't really seem to notice them at all. Sitting right between
the eyes, the boys decided to tickle him to see just what would happen.
They tickled the smooth skin, but nothing seemed to happen.

"Maybe we need to tickle him a little more!" Jon yelled over to Max.
With both hands, the boys tickled and tickled the top of the
dinosaur's nose. Suddenly the dinosaur wasn't still anymore.
The head tilted back as the body of the huge Diplodocus
wiggled with excitement.
The boys slid down the long neck like a rollercoaster.
Down the neck and past the body, the boys were caught by the tail.
The Diplodocus wrapped his tail around the boys and tickled them.

"AHHHHH, I can't take it anymore!"
Jon giggled looking over at Max.

"How do we stop it?
I CAN'T FEEL MY STOMACH!" Max laughed.
"Let's open the book!" Jon grabbed the book from his backpack and opened it quickly. In a matter of seconds, the boys found themselves by a rainforest with bright, beautiful flowers.

"What does the book say now?" Max looked over.
The pages in the book flipped to another terrifying dinosaur.
"My looks may be striking; see if you can strike me out."

A few seconds of silence fell over the boys.
"BASEBALL?!!" They screamed!
"Let's get him," Jon said excitedly, pulling out the map.
The boys ran through the rainforest to the location of Ankylosaurus Field.

"We must be close. Do you hear the loud thuds?" Max said.
The boys stepped on the field and the huge dinosaur turned to
lock eyes with them. He then walked over to a
brown ball about the size of a baseball,
maybe a little bigger. He hit the ball across the field to the
feet of the boys as they stood watching in amazement.
Soon, the boys were playing baseball with an Ankylosaurus.

"Time for a new mission, I think." Max said.
After playing with the Ankylosaurus, the boys found themselves
exploring places all over the map.
The boys played drums with an Allosaurus as
he showed off his dance moves with his huge feet.
The Dimorphodon flew high in the sky and gave the boys a bird,
well dinosaur, eye view of the entire jungle.

"Jon... Jon, hey buddy.
It's time to meet your mama and sisters for lunch."
Jon felt like he was being shaken from a deep dream.
Pulling at the 3D glasses,
Jon looked up and saw his Dad.
"You okay, son?"

"Oh yea, sorry, Dad.
How long have we been sitting here?"
Jon looks over at Max, who is also taking off his 3D glasses.
"A little over an hour. This book must be very interesting."
Dad laughed as he helped the boys gather their things.
"Oh yea, DEFINITELY!" The boys looked at each other.

"Can I get the book so Max can come over sometime?"
Jon looked up to his Dad excitedly.
"Sure thing. I also got a couple of books I think you would enjoy."
Dad held out the books he picked while
Jon and Max were deep in the jungle with dinosaurs.

"Oh, wow! Thanks, Mr. Williams!" Max exclaimed.
"Thanks, Dad!" Jon laughed.
"No problem, boys." Dad smiled.

Later that night, Jon had a new excitement for books.
Although the story Dad read didn't come to life like Dino Explore,
Jon enjoyed bedtime stories again.
His imagination was brightened and restored from the encounter
he had in the jungles of Dino Explore.

Made in the USA
Coppell, TX
12 January 2021